TIME FOR BED

Mem Fox

TIME FOR BED

ILLUSTRATED BY

Jane Dyer

ISBN 0-590-13833-2

12 11 10 9 8 7 6   0 1/0

Printed in the U.S.A.

The paintings in this book were done in Winsor & Newton
watercolors on Waterford 140-lb. hot-press paper.
The display type and text type were set in Goudy Old Style.
Designed by Camilla Filancia.

For Allyn and Louise,
because this book needs two more stars

—M. F.

And for Barry,
because this book needs a bear

—J. D.

It's time for bed, little mouse, little mouse,
Darkness is falling all over the house.

It's time for bed, little goose, little goose,
The stars are out and on the loose.

It's time for bed, little cat, little cat,
So snuggle in tight, that's right, like that.

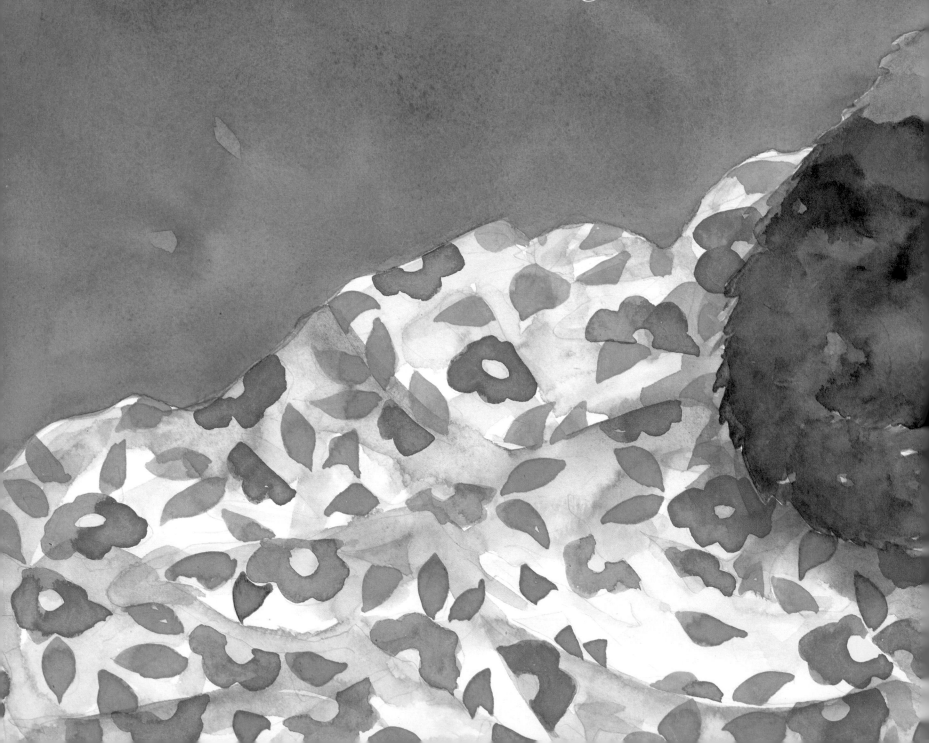

It's time for bed, little calf, little calf,
What happened today that made you laugh?

It's time for bed, little foal, little foal,
I'll whisper a secret, but don't tell a soul.

It's time for bed, little fish, little fish,
So hold your breath and make a wish.

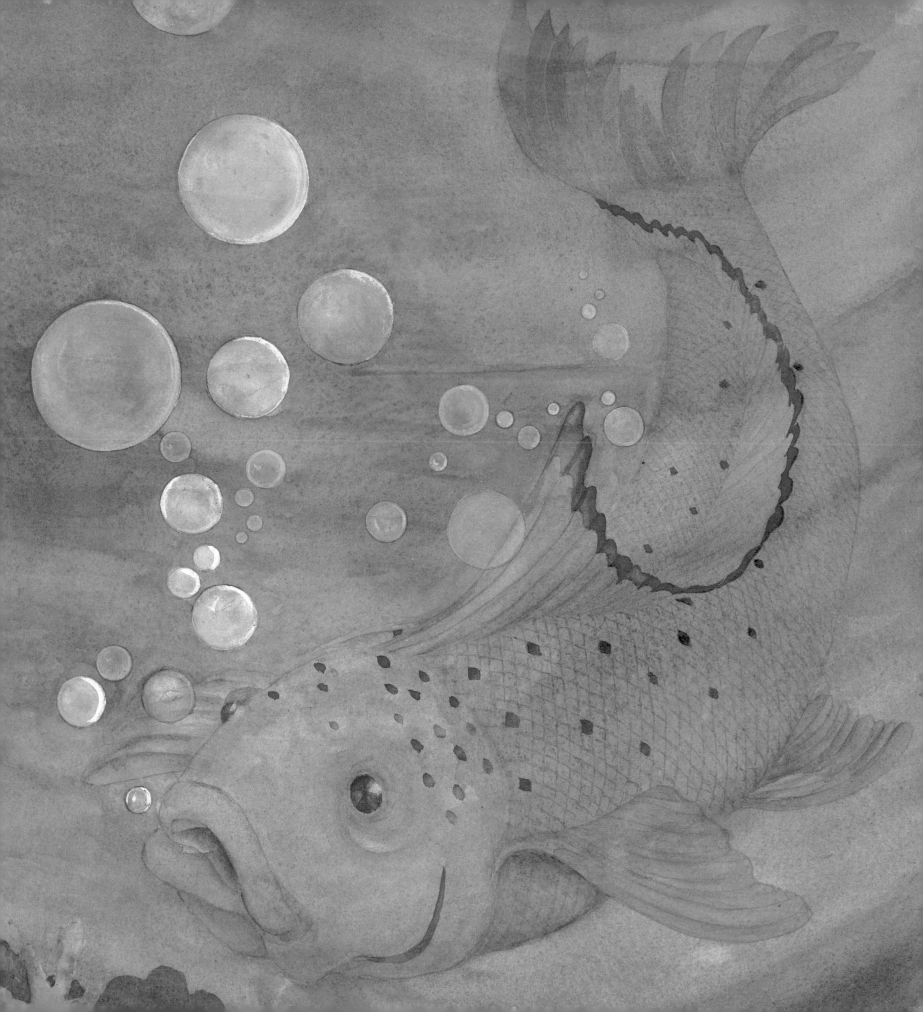

It's time for bed, little sheep, little sheep,
The whole wide world is going to sleep.

It's time to sleep, little bird, little bird,
So close your eyes, not another word.

It's time to sleep, little bee, little bee,
Yes, I love you and you love me.

It's time to sleep, little snake, little snake,
Good gracious me, you're still awake!

It's time to sleep, little pup, little pup,
If you don't sleep soon the sun will be up!

It's time to sleep, little deer, little deer,
The very last kiss is almost here.

The stars on high are shining bright—
Sweet dreams, my darling, sleep well . . .

good night!